W9-COR-981

Pinkerton, Behave!

Story and pictures by

STEVEN KELLOGG

Dial Books for Young Readers · New York

Published by
Dial Books for Young Readers
2 Park Avenue
New York, New York 10016
Copyright © 1979 by Steven Kellogg
All rights reserved
Library of Congress Catalog Card Number: 78-31794
First Pied Piper Printing 1982
Printed in Hong Kong by South China Printing Co.
COBE
6 8 10 9 7

A Pied Piper Book is a registered trademark of
Dial Books for Young Readers
® TM 1,163,686 and ® TM 1,054,312

PINKERTON, BEHAVE!
is published in a hardcover edition by
Dial Books for Young Readers.
ISBN 0-8037-7250-5

For Helen,
my best friend and
the person who chose
the Great Pinkerton

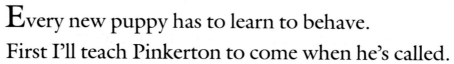

Every new puppy has to learn to behave.
First I'll teach Pinkerton to come when he's called.

Come!

He can learn to bring us the newspaper.

Fetch!

From now on *I'll* fetch the newspaper.

But it's important for him to defend the house if a burglar comes.

We'll pretend this dummy is a burglar.

Get the burglar, Pinkerton!

I think we need some professional help.
Pinkerton will have to go to obedience school.

When this poor creature sees how well the other dogs behave, he will understand what we expect of him.

We begin with a simple command. Come.

COME! COME! COME!

We cannot hold back the entire class for one confused student.
On to the next lesson!

Every dog must fetch the evening paper.

Fetch, you fleabrain, FETCH!

Our next lesson is a most important one.
Get the burglar!

Pinkerton sets a poor example for the rest of the class.
Unless he shows some improvement, he will be dismissed.

We will now review all that we have learned.
Dogs! Pay attention!

COME!

FETCH!

GET THE BURGLAR!

OUT! OUT! OUT! OUT!

Mom, you and Pinkerton look pretty tired.
Why don't you go to bed and get a good night's rest?

Pleasant dreams, Pinkerton.

This is a stickup, lady. Don't move, or I'll blast you and your silly hound to chicken powder.

Psssssst! Pinkerton! A burglar!

I warned you, lady.

Pinkerton! Fetch!

GRRRRRRRRRRRRR

Pinkerton! Come!

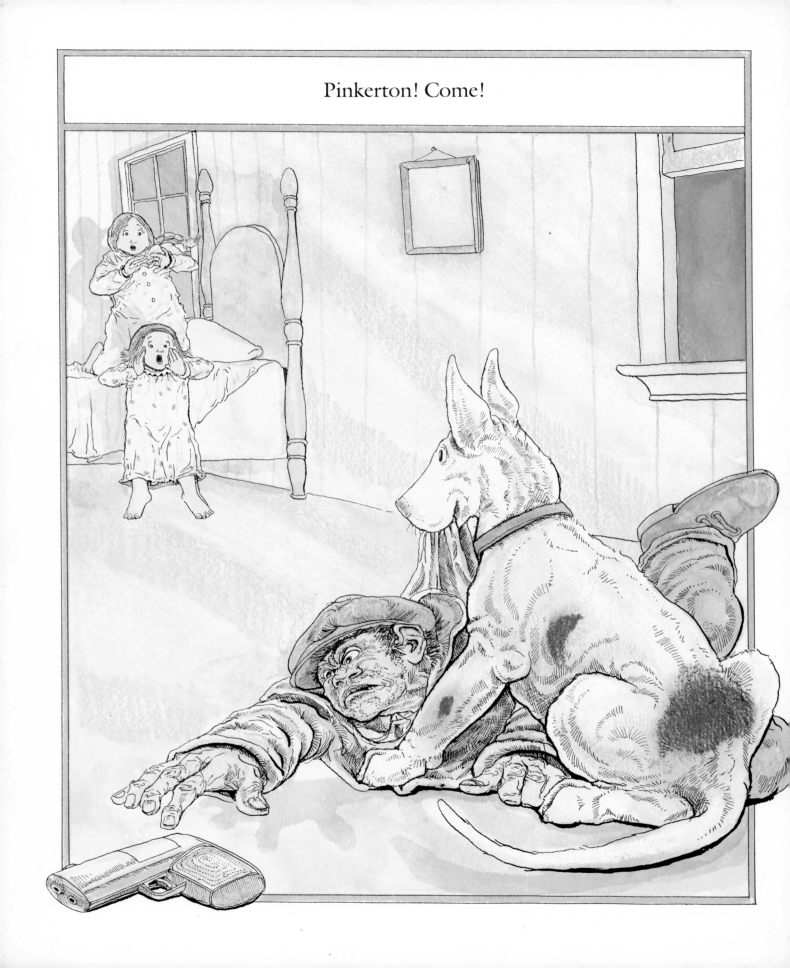

Pinkerton, I'm a burglar.

I love you, Pinkerton.